HOME ON THE RANGE

SMITHSONIAN INSTITUTION

To Dayton Hyde, whose Black Hills Wild Horse Sanctuary inspired this book's background scenes and in whose childhood home we now live.—D.M.

Book design: Konrad Krukowski
Editor: Barbie Heit Schwaeber
Production Editor: Brian E. Giblin

First Edition 2007
10 9 8 7 6 5 4 3 2 1
Printed in China

Acknowledgments:
    Soundprints would like to thank Ellen Nanney and Katie Mann at the Smithsonian Institution's Office of Product Development and Licensing for their help in the creation of this book.

   A portion of the proceeds from your purchase of this licensed product supports the stated educational mission of the Smithsonian Institution - "the increase and diffusion of knowledge."

Library of Congress Cataloging-in-Publication Data is on file with the publisher and the Library of Congress.

HOME ON THE RANGE

Edited by Barbie H. Schwaeber
Illustrated by Diana Magnuson

Soundprints
Where Children Discover...

Oh, give me a home

where the buffalo roam,

Where the deer
and the antelope play;

Where seldom is heard
a discouraging word,

And the skies are not cloudy all day.

Home,
home on the range

Where the deer and the antelope play;

Where seldom is heard

a discouraging word,

And the skies are not cloudy all day.

NOTES AND NOSTALGIA

The song "Home on the Range" was first written as a poem called "My Western Home" in 1872. It was written by Dr. Brewster M. Higley, a settler on the Kansas prairie. The simplicity of the western pioneer life and the beauty of the blue skies were his inspiration.

Dr. Higley moved to Kansas in 1871. He left his career as a physician in Indiana to stake a claim on a small plot of land as part of the Homestead Act of 1862. As the story goes, a local Kansas prairie man named Trube Reese was visiting Higley and saw the poem lying on a desk in his cabin. He convinced Higley to turn it into a song. Higley chose Daniel E. Kelly, a fiddler from a local musical group to create the music. A few friends then helped Higley improve the lyrics. The song quickly caught on and spread across the country, with the lyrics adapting easily from one location to another.

In the early 1900's, John Lomax, a man well-known for telling folk tales, took a liking to the tune and recorded a saloonkeeper in Texas singing a version of the song. This version was eventually published in Lomax's book, "Cowboy Songs & Other Frontier Ballads." It soon became a national favorite.

In 1927, "Home on the Range" turned out to be a smash hit for Texas singer, Vernon Dalhardt. It was his version that launched the song into the popularity it still enjoys today. Over the years, it has been recorded by many singers and enjoyed by people all across the country. President Franklin Roosevelt even announced that it was his favorite song in the early 1930's.

Today, this classic folk song we all know so well serves as the official song of the state of Kansas. The chorus to this well-known version is adapted from Higley's original song. The lyrics used in this book are from "Cowboy Songs & Other Frontier Ballads," first copy written in 1910.

HOME ON THE RANGE

On March 21, 1874, a local Kansas newspaper called the *Kirwin Chief* published the words to "Western Home" as originally written by Dr. Brewster Higley. See if you can find how these lyrics differ from the song as we sing it today.

Western Home

Oh! Give me a home where the buffalo roam,
Where the deer and the antelope play;
Where never is heard a discouraging word,
And the sky is not clouded all day.

(Chorus) A home! A home!
Where the deer and antelope play,
Where seldom is heard a discouraging word,
And the sky is not clouded all day.

Oh! Give me land where the bright diamond sand
Throws its light from the glittering streams,
Where glideth along the graceful white swan,
Like the maid in her heavenly dreams.

(Chorus) A home! A home!
Where the deer and antelope play,
Where seldom is heard a discouraging word,
And the sky is not clouded all day.

Oh! Give me a gale of the Solomon vale,
Where the life streams with buoyancy flow;
Or the banks of the Beaver, where seldom if ever,
Any poisonous herbage doth grow.

(Chorus) A home! A home!
Where the deer and antelope play,
Where seldom is heard a discouraging word,
And the sky is not clouded all day.

How often at night, when the heavens were bright
With the light of twinkling stars,
Have I stood here amazed and asked as I gazed
If their glory exceed that of ours.

(Chorus) A home! A home!
Where the deer and antelope play,
Where seldom is heard a discouraging word,
And the sky is not clouded all day.

I love the wild flowers in this bright land of ours
I love the wild curlew's shrill scream;
The bluffs and white rocks, and antelope flocks
That graze on the mountains so green.

(Chorus) A home! A home!
Where the deer and antelope play,
Where seldom is heard a discouraging word,
And the sky is not clouded all day.

The air is so pure and the breezes so free,
The zephyrs so balmy and light,
That I would not exchange my home here to range
Forever in azure so bright.

(Chorus) A home! A home!
Where the deer and antelope play,
Where seldom is heard a discouraging word,
And the sky is not clouded all day.